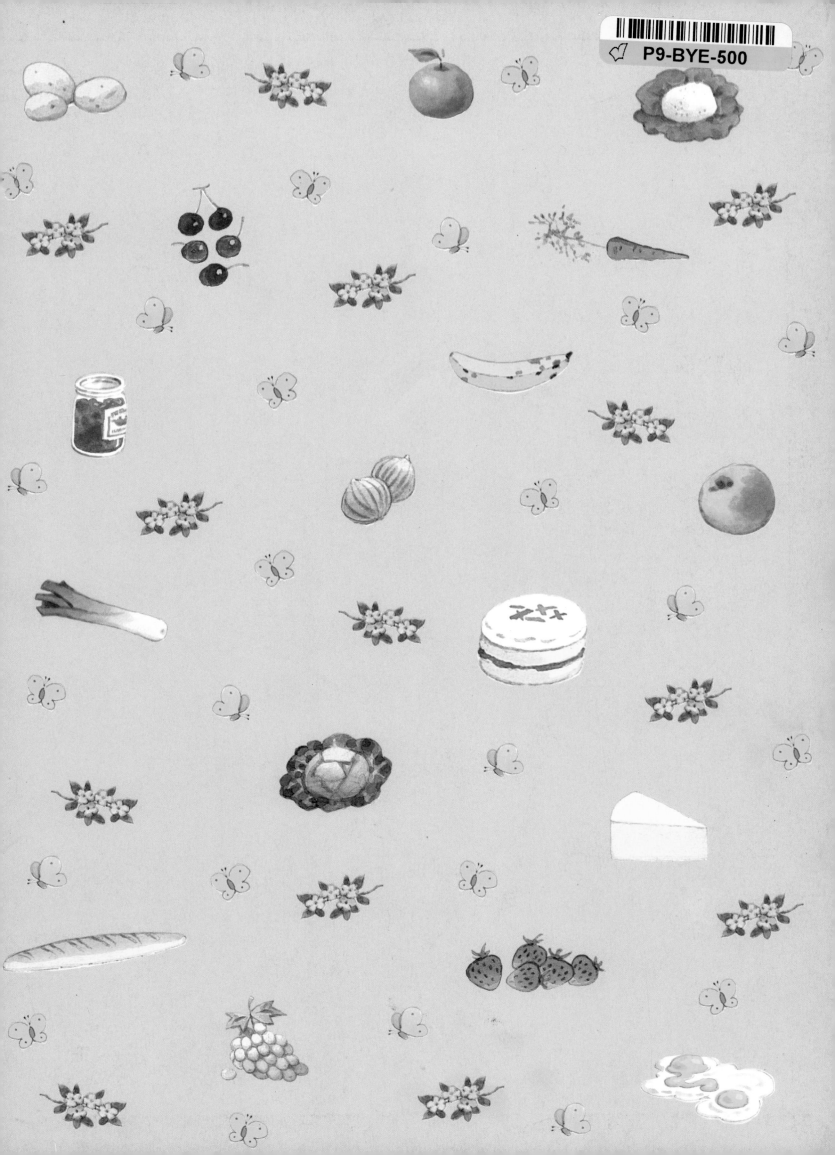

The Usborne
Farmyard Tales
Children's Cookbook

Fiona Watt

Illustrated by Stephen Cartwright
and Molly Sage

Recipes by Catherine Atkinson, Roz Denny

and Julia Kirby Jones

Designed by Helen Wood

Photography by Howard Allman

American editor - Carrie Seay
American expert - Barbara Trincella

There is a little yellow duck to find on every double page.

This is Apple Tree Farm.

Mr. Boot and Mrs. Boot live here with their two children, Poppy and Sam. They have a dog called Rusty and a cat called Whiskers. Ted drives the tractor and helps look after all the animals on the farm.

Contents

Below each list of ingredients, you can find out how long each recipe will keep. Some of them need to be eaten on the day they are made, but others will keep for a few days. If you're not sure of some of the cooking words, turn to pages 46-47 where you will find tips and explanations to help you.

Cheese and tomato tarts

Makes six tarts

13oz. package of puff pastry
1 tablespoon of milk
1 large onion
3 tablespoons of olive oil
half a teaspoon of Italian seasoning
salt and ground black pepper
8oz. cherry tomatoes
8oz. Mozzarella cheese

Preheat your oven to 425°F.

Eat the tarts after they have cooled for a few minutes.

Trim the pastry to fit the baking sheet.

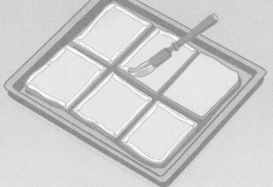

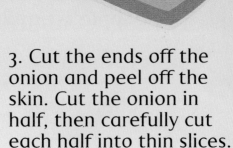

1. Turn on your oven. Unroll the pastry and put it on a baking sheet. Trim one end off if you need to, then cut it into six pieces.

2. Put the milk into a cup. Use a pastry brush to brush the milk around the edges of the pieces, to make a ½in. border.

3. Cut the ends off the onion and peel off the skin. Cut the onion in half, then carefully cut each half into thin slices.

If you like olives, scatter one or two on each tart with the tomatoes.

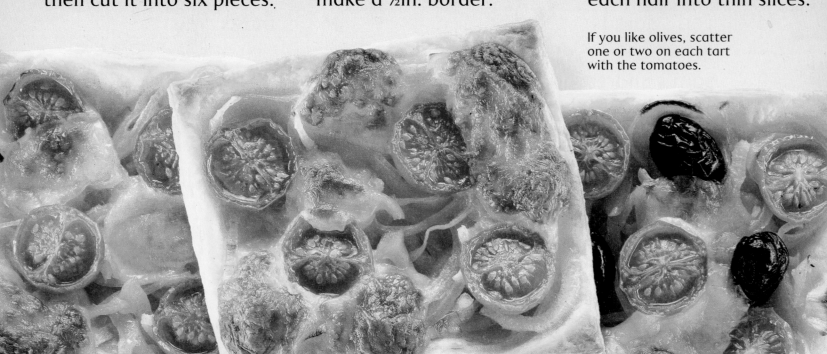

You can also add zucchini to these tarts.

Slice a medium zucchini and add it to the pan, halfway through cooking the onion at step 4.

4. Heat the olive oil over a low heat and add the pieces of onion. Cook gently for ten minutes until the onion is soft.

5. Stir in the Italian seasoning and some salt and pepper and stir. Spoon the onion over the pastry, but do not cover the milky border.

6. Use a serrated knife to cut the tomatoes in half. Arrange the tomatoes on top of the mixture, with their cut sides upward.

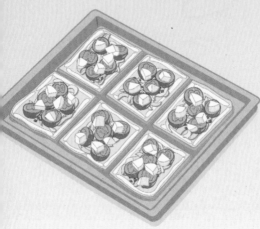

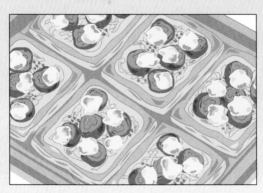

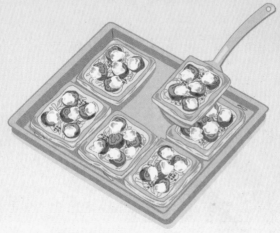

7. Open the package of Mozzarella. Cut the cheese into ½in. cubes. Scatter them evenly over the tomatoes.

8. Put the baking sheet on the middle shelf of the oven for 25-30 minutes, until the pastry rises and turns brown.

9. Leave the tarts on the baking sheet for about three minutes to cool a little. Then, serve the tarts immediately.

Marshmallow crispies

Makes about 12 pieces

4oz. toffee
½ cup butter or margarine
2 cups marshmallows
7 cups puffed rice cereal

a 11 x 7in. shallow pan

Storage: Keep in an airtight container and eat within four days.

They will take about 15 minutes to melt.

1. Grease the pan with butter on a paper towel. If you have a slab of toffee, put it in a plastic bag and break it up with a rolling pin.

2. Put the toffee and butter or margarine into a pan. Add the marshmallows. Melt them gently over a low heat, stirring all the time.

3. When everything has melted and blended together, take the pan off the heat. Gently stir in the rice cereal.

4. Spoon the mixture into the pan and press it gently with the back of a metal spoon. Leave the mixture to set, then cut it up.

Cornflake crunch

Makes eight pieces

8oz. semi-sweet chocolate bar
or chips
3 tablespoons of white corn syrup
4 tablespoons margarine
5 cups cornflakes

8in. shallow pan

 Storage: Keep in an airtight
container and eat within four days.

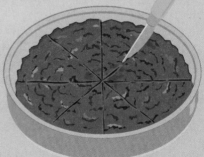

1. Grease the pan with a
little butter or margarine
on a paper towel. Grease
the inside well, but do not
leave on too much butter.

2. Break the chocolate into
a large pan. Add the syrup
and margarine. Heat the
pan gently, stirring the
mixture all the time.

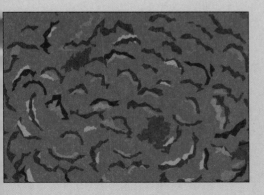

Lift the pieces out with a
blunt knife or a pie knife.

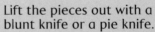

3. When the chocolate has
melted, add the cornflakes
and stir them well. Make
sure that they are coated
all over with chocolate.

4. Spoon the mixture
into the pan. Carefully
smooth the top with the
back of a spoon. Try not
to crush the cornflakes.

5. Put the pan in the
refrigerator to set. It will
take about two hours.
Then, use a sharp knife to
cut it into eight pieces.

Poppy's tasty pancakes

Makes about 12 pancakes

1 cup all-purpose flour
a pinch of salt
1 egg
3 tablespoons of vegetable oil, divided
1 cup of milk

You can leave the pancake mixture until you are ready to use it, but stir it before making your pancakes. Eat them immediately.

Use a whisk to beat it.

1. Put a sifter over a large mixing bowl. Pour in the flour and the salt. Shake the sifter until all the flour has fallen through.

2. Press a whisk into the middle of the flour to make a deep hollow. Break an egg into a cup, then pour it into the hollow.

3. Add a tablespoon of oil and two tablespoons of milk. Beat the egg, oil and milk with some of the flour from around the hollow.

Eat the pancakes with maple syrup, or lemon juice and sugar. You can also spread them with honey, chocolate spread or jam.

4. Add some more milk and beat it again. Continue to add some milk and beat it, until all the milk is mixed in and the batter is smooth.

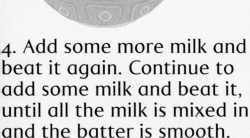

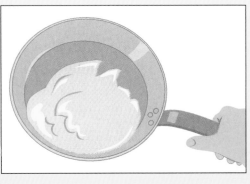

5. Heat a small frying pan over a medium heat for about a minute. Don't put anything into the pan at this point.

6. Put two tablespoons of oil into a cup. Roll up a paper towel and dip one end into it. Wipe oil quickly over the bottom of the pan.

7. Quickly add three tablespoons of batter. Swirl it all over the bottom by tipping the pan. The batter should sizzle.

Make a stack of pancakes under the towel.

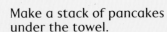

8. Put the pan on the heat and cook the batter until it turns pale and is lightly cooked. Small holes will also appear on the top.

9. Loosen the edge of the pancake and slide a spatula under it. Flip the pancake over and cook it for half a minute more.

10. Slide the pancake onto a plate, then cover it with a clean towel. Make more pancakes, following steps 6 to 9.

Farmyard cookies

Makes about 18 cookies

2 cups flour
2 teaspoons of ground ginger
2 teaspoons baking soda
½ cup butter
½ cup soft light brown sugar
½ cup white sugar
1 egg
4 tablespoons of maple syrup

large farm animal cookie
  cutters

Preheat your oven to 350°F.

🦋 Storage: Keep in an airtight
container and eat within five days.

1. Dip a paper towel in
some margarine and rub
it over two baking sheets
to grease them. Then,
turn on your oven.

2. Sift the flour, ginger
and baking soda into a
mixing bowl. Cut the
butter into chunks and
add it to the bowl.

3. Rub the butter into the
flour with your fingertips,
until the mixture looks like
fine breadcrumbs. Stir in
the sugar and brown sugar.

4. Break the egg into a
small bowl. Add the syrup
to the egg, then use a
fork to beat them
together well.

5. Stir the eggy mixture
into the flour. Mix
everything together with
a metal spoon until it
makes a soft dough.

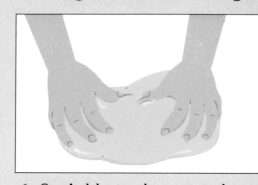

6. Sprinkle a clean work
surface with flour and put
the dough onto it. Stretch
the dough by pushing it
away from you.

7. Fold the dough in half. Turn it and push it away from you again. Continue to push, turn and fold until the dough is smooth.

8. Cut the dough in half. Sprinkle a little more flour onto your work surface. Roll out the dough until it is about ¼in. thick.

9. Use cookie cutters to cut out lots of shapes from the dough. Then, lift the shapes onto the baking sheets with a spatula.

10. Roll out the other half of dough and cut shapes from it. Squeeze the scraps to make a ball. Roll it out and cut more shapes.

Spread the shapes out on the baking sheets.

11. Put the the baking sheets into your oven and bake them for 12-15 minutes. They will turn golden brown.

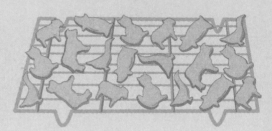

12. Leave the cookies on the sheets for about five minutes. Then, lift them onto a wire rack. Leave them to cool.

Sam and Poppy's muffins

Makes 12 muffins

2¼ cups self-rising flour
pinch of salt
1 teaspoon of baking powder
¼ cup butter
½ cup soft light brown sugar
1 cup (4oz.) chocolate chips
2 eggs
2 teaspoons of vanilla extract
1 cup of milk

muffin tins

Preheat your oven to 400°F.

Eat immediately, or keep in an airtight container and eat within three days.

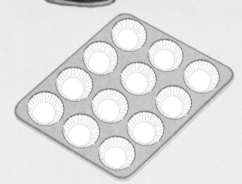

1. Dip a paper towel into some butter or margarine and rub it inside the holes in the tin. Then, put a paper muffin case in each hole.

2. Turn on your oven. Put a sifter over a large bowl. Then, shake the flour, salt and baking powder through the sifter.

3. Cut the butter into small pieces and add it to the flour mixture. Rub the butter into the flour until it looks like breadcrumbs.

4. Add the light brown sugar and about three-quarters of the chocolate chips. Stir them in until they are mixed in evenly.

5. Break the eggs into a medium-sized bowl and beat them with a fork. Add the vanilla and milk, then beat it again.

6. Pour the egg mixture into the flour all at once. Mix it quickly with a fork to blend everything. It should still look a little lumpy.

7. Spoon some mixture into each paper case, filling it almost to the top. Sprinkle the remaining chocolate chips on top.

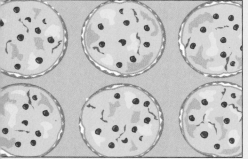

8. Bake the muffins in the oven for about 20 minutes until the muffins have risen in the paper cases and the tops are firm.

9. Leave the muffins in the tin for about five minutes, then lift them onto a wire rack. Serve them while they are still warm.

For double chocolate muffins, use 2 cups of self-rising flour and 3 tablespoons of cocoa powder.

Sam's favorite soup

Serves four to six

2 medium potatoes
2 medium leeks or 4 green onions
2 tablespoons butter
1 tablespoon of cooking oil
1 vegetable bouillon cube
dried seasonings
¼ cup of milk
salt and ground black pepper
parsley

Eat immediately.

1. Use a vegetable peeler to peel the potatoes. Then, cut the peeled pieces into small chunks. Put them into a large pan.

2. Cut the roots and the dark green tops off the leeks. Slice through the outside layer of each leek, then peel it off.

3. Wash the leeks thoroughly under cold running water. Make sure that there is no dirt left between the layers.

4. Slice the leeks into ½in. pieces. Put the leeks, butter and oil into the pan with the potatoes and stir everything well.

5. Turn on the heat and slowly melt the butter. When it starts to sizzle, put a lid on the pan and turn the heat down low.

6. Let the vegetables cook gently for ten minutes. Shake the pan occasionally to stop it from sticking, but don't lift the lid.

...tir until the vegetable cube dissolves.

7. Meanwhile, boil some water. Put the vegetable cube into a measuring cup. Pour in 4 cups of boiling water and stir it.

8. When the vegetables are cooked, carefully pour in the stock. Add a pinch of dried seasonings, the milk and a little salt and pepper.

9. Turn up the heat and bring the soup to the boil. Then, turn the heat down so that the soup is bubbling gently.

...o. Let the soup cook for about 15 minutes more. Then, use a ladle to serve the soup immediately into bowls.

...prinkle each bowl of soup with some chopped parsley and serve it with warm bread rolls (see pages 44-45).

Delicious lemon cake

Makes about 12 slices

a lemon
2 cups self-rising flour
1 teaspoon baking powder
4 eggs
¾ cup soft margarine
1 cup sugar

For the filling:
½ cup sugar
2 eggs
a lemon
4 tablespoons unsalted butter

For the icing:
a lemon
1 cup powdered sugar

Two 7in. round tins

Preheat your oven to 350°F.

✺ Storage: this is best eaten on the day it is made, but you can store it for up to two days in airtight container in the refrigerator.

1. Draw around the pans on greaseproof or wax paper. Cut out the circles and put them in the pans. Grease the pans.

2. Turn on your oven. Grate the rind off a lemon, then cut it in half. Twist each half on a lemon squeezer to squeeze out the juice.

3. Sift the flour and baking powder into a bowl. Break the eggs into a cup, then add them, along with the margarine and sugar.

4. Beat everything in the bowl well, then stir in the lemon rind and lemon juice. Divide the mixture between the two pans.

5. Bake the cakes for 25 minutes, until they spring up when you press them in the middle. Then, leave them on a rack to cool.

6. While the cakes are cooling, make the filling. Put the sugar into a heatproof bowl. Break the eggs and add them.

7. Grate the rind off a lemon and squeeze the juice from it. Add the rind and juice to the bowl. Cut the butter into pieces and add it, too.

8. Put some water into a pan and turn on the heat so that the water begins to bubble. Lower the bowl into the pan.

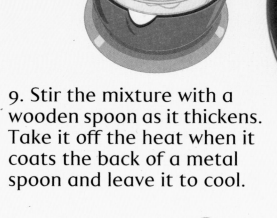

9. Stir the mixture with a wooden spoon as it thickens. Take it off the heat when it coats the back of a metal spoon and leave it to cool.

10. Spread one of the cakes with the filling. Put the other cake carefully on top. Don't worry if some of the filling oozes out.

A zester gives you long pieces of rind.

Press hard as you scrape.

11. Grate some rind off the remaining lemon, or scrape some off with a zester. Keep the rind on one side for decorating the cake.

Stir in the juice a little at a time.

12. To make the icing, squeeze half of the lemon. Sift the powdered sugar. Pour in the juice until it is like glue. Ice and decorate the cake.

Poppy's 'pizzas'

Serves two

1 onion
2 cloves of garlic
2 tablespoons of olive oil
15oz. can of chopped tomatoes
half a teaspoon of Italian seasoning
salt and ground black pepper
1 ciabatta bread
9oz. Mozzarella cheese
2 tablespoons of grated Parmesan cheese
a selection of toppings such as ham, olives,
    pepperoni, salami, cherry tomatoes

Preheat your oven to 400°F.

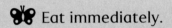 Eat immediately.

1. Cut the top and bottom off the onion and peel the skin off it. Cut it in half and slice it. Peel the garlic cloves and crush them.

2. Heat the oil in a frying pan. Gently cook the garlic and onion, for five minutes, or until they are soft, stirring once or twice.

3. Add the tomatoes, the seasoning and some salt and pepper. Turn up the heat and bring the mixture to the boil.

4. Turn the heat down to medium and let the mixture cook for about ten minutes, or until most of the liquid has gone.

5. Take the frying pan off the heat. Leave the mixture to cool for 10-15 minutes. Meanwhile, turn on your oven to heat up.

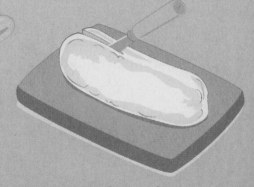

6. Put the bread onto a chopping board and cut it in half lengthways. Put the two halves onto a large baking sheet.

7. Spread each piece of bread with the topping. Slice the Mozzarella cheese as finely as you can and lay the slices on top.

8. Add any other toppings you want, then sprinkle Parmesan cheese on top. Bake the 'pizzas' for about 15 minutes.

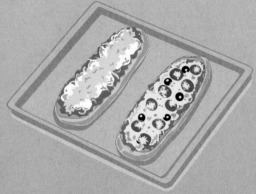

9. Take the baking sheet out of the oven and let the 'pizzas' cool for five minutes. Cut each half into pieces, to make it easier to eat.

Try one with cheese, pepperoni and olives.

Apple crumble

Serves six

3-4 eating apples
6 tablespoons of water
ground cinnamon
1 tablespoon of sugar

For the topping:
1 cup all-purpose flour
1 cup whole-wheat flour
¾ cup butter
⅔ cup light soft brown sugar

Preheat your oven to 350°F.

✿ This is best served hot and eaten immediately.

1. Cut the apples into quarters. Peel them, then cut out the cores. Cut the pieces into chunks. Put them in a casserole dish.

2. Add the water. Sprinkle the apples with a large pinch of cinnamon and a tablespoon of sugar. Turn on your oven.

3. Stir both types of flour together in a mixing bowl. Then, cut the butter into small pieces and put it in the bowl with the flour.

4. Mix the flour and butter with a blunt knife. Stir and cut the flour again and again until each piece of butter is coated with flour.

5. Wash your hands and dry them really well. Rub the butter into the flour. Lift the mixture and let it fall as you rub.

6. When the mixture looks like coarse breadcrumbs, mix in the brown sugar. Mix it in with your fingers, too.

You could use plums or blackberries instead of apples to make this crumble.

7. Sprinkle the topping over the apple. Spread it out evenly with a fork and smooth the top. Put the dish onto a baking sheet.

8. Bake the crumble for 45 minutes, until the top is golden. Turn the crumble around halfway through, so that it browns evenly.

9. To check that it is cooked, push a knife into a piece of apple. If it's not soft, cook the crumble for five more minutes.

10. Leave the crumble to cool for at least five minutes before you serve it. Serve it with whipped cream or ice cream.

Mrs. Boot's special cherry loaf

Makes about eight slices

5oz. Maraschino cherries
1¾ cups self-rising flour
¾ cup butter, softened
¾ cup sugar
2oz. almonds, finely chopped*
3 eggs

a loaf pan measuring
  8 x 5 x 3½in.

Preheat your oven to 350°F.

✿ Storage : the cake will keep
for four days if you wrap it in wax
paper, then in foil or put it in an
airtight container.

Instead of cherries you could use
other dried fruit, such as dried
apricots.

* Don't give this cake to anyone
who is allergic to nuts

Use kitchen scissors
to cut the cherries.

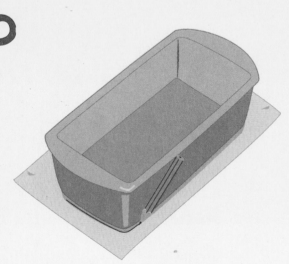

1. Cut each cherry into
quarters. Put them in a
strainer and rinse them under
warm running water. Pat
them dry on a paper towel.

2. Put the loaf pan onto
greaseproof or wax paper.
Draw around the bottom
of the pan and cut out the
shape.

3. Grease the bottom and
sides of the pan with some
margarine on a paper
towel. Put the paper into
the tin. Turn on your oven.

4. Sift the flour into a bowl. Add the butter, sugar and chopped almonds. Break the eggs into a cup, then pour them in too.

5. Beat the mixture firmly with a wooden spoon, until it is light and fluffy. Gently fold in the pieces of cherry with a metal spoon.

6. Scrape the mixture out of the bowl into the loaf pan. Smooth the top with the back of a spoon to make it level.

When you slice the cake, the cherries are scattered through each piece.

7. Bake the loaf for about 1¼ hours, until it rises and turns golden. Leave it for a few minutes, then turn it onto a wire rack.

8. When the cake is completely cold, put it onto a cutting board. Use a bread knife to cut it into about eight slices.

Ted's salads

Each salad serves four

For the lemon and honey dressing:
5 tablespoons of vegetable oil
1½ tablespoons of lemon juice
1 teaspoon of light honey
salt and ground black pepper

For the potato salad:
1½lbs. small new potatoes
2 sticks of celery
2 small red-skinned dessert apples
6 stems of fresh chives

For the garden salad:
2 little, or baby, gem lettuces
half a cucumber
8oz. plum or cherry
tomatoes
2 medium carrots

Eat immediately.

Lemon and honey dressing

Put the lid on the jar before you shake it.

For the dressing, put the oil, lemon juice, honey and a pinch of salt and pepper into a jar which has a screw top. Shake it well.

Potato salad

Wait until the potatoes are cool enough to handle.

1. For the potato salad, scrub the potatoes. Boil them for about 15 minutes, until they are cooked. Drain them and cut them into smaller pieces.

Leave the rest of the dressing in the jar.

2. Put the potatoes in a large bowl, and pour half of the dressing over them while they are still warm. Leave them to cool.

Garden salad

3. Wash the celery and slice it into thin slices. Cut the apples into quarters and cut out the cores. Cut the apples into small chunks.

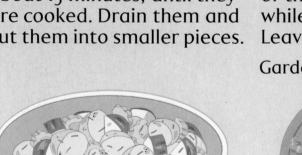

4. Using kitchen scissors, snip the chives into small pieces. Add the celery, apples and chives to the bowl. Mix everything well.

1. For the garden salad, pull the leaves off the lettuce. Rinse them well, shake them dry, then tear them into pieces.

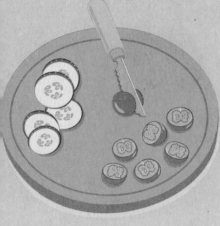

2. Put the lettuce leaves in a large bowl. Slice the cucumber finely. Use a serrated knife to cut the tomatoes in half.

Serve the salads in a big bowl or as individual portions on plates.

3. Peel the carrots and cut them in half. Then, cut them into very thin strips. Add the tomatoes, carrots and cucumber to the bowl.

4. Shake the rest of the dressing in the jar, and pour it over the garden salad. Then, gently mix everything together.

Sam's shortbread

Makes eight pieces

1½ cups flour
½ cup butter, refrigerated
¼ cup sugar

An 8in. shallow round pan

Preheat your oven to 325°F.

 Storage: keep in an airtight container and eat within five days.

1. Turn on your oven to heat it up. Dip a paper towel into some butter, then rub it over the inside of the pan.

2. Put a sifter over a large mixing bowl and pour the flour into it. Shake the sifter so that the flour falls into the bowl.

3. Cut the butter into small pieces and put them into the bowl. Mix the pieces with a blunt knife to coat them with flour.

4. Rub the pieces of butter between your fingertips. Lift the mixture and let it fall back into the bowl as you rub.

5. Continue rubbing in the butter until the mixture looks like breadcrumbs. Stir in the sugar with a wooden spoon.

6. Holding the bowl in one hand, squeeze the mixture into a ball. The heat from your hand will make the mixture stick together.

Cut across it again, before lifting it out.

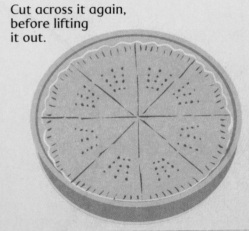

7. Press the mixture into the pan with your fingers, then use the back of a spoon to press down the top and make it level.

8. Use the prongs of a fork to press a pattern around the edge. Then, cut the mixture into eight equal pieces with a blunt knife.

9. Bake it for 30 minutes, until it becomes golden. Leave the shortbread for five minutes before putting it on a wire rack.

Mrs. Boot's best carrot cake

Makes 8 to 12 slices

3 medium carrots ✓
¾ cup butter ✓
2 large eggs
1¼ cups light soft brown sugar ✓
1⅔ cups self-rising flour ✓
half a teaspoon of salt ✓
2 teaspoons of ground cinnamon ✓
2 teaspoons of baking powder ✓
¾ cup chopped walnuts* ✓
2 tablespoons of milk

For the frosting:
2 cups powdered sugar ✓
7oz. cream cheese
1 tablespoon of lemon juice
half a teaspoon of vanilla extract ✓

a 7 x 11in. shallow cake tin

Preheat your oven to 350°F.

🦋 Storage: keep in a sealed container in the refrigerator and eat within three days.

* Don't give these to anyone who is allergic to nuts.

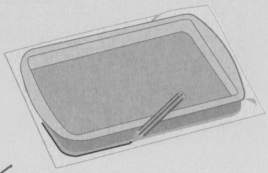

1. Put your cake pan onto a piece of greaseproof or wax paper and draw around it. Cut out the shape you have drawn.

2. Brush the sides and the base of pan with a little vegetable oil to grease it. Put the paper inside and brush it with oil, too.

3. Turn on your oven. Wash the carrots and cut off their tops. Grate them on the side of the grater with the biggest holes.

4. Put the butter into a pan and heat it gently until it has just melted. Pour the melted butter into a large bowl.

5. Break the eggs into a small bowl and beat them. Stir the carrots and sugar into the melted butter. Then, add the beaten eggs.

6. Put a sifter over the bowl. Shake the flour, salt, cinnamon and baking powder through the sifter, onto the mixture.

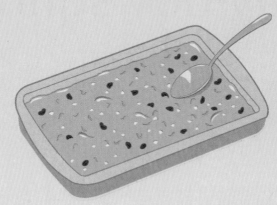

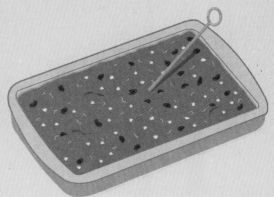

7. Use a wooden spoon to beat the mixture, until it is smooth. Add the walnuts, then stir in the two tablespoons of milk.

8. Spoon the mixture into the pan. Smooth the top with a spoon. Tap the pan on your work surface to make the mixture level.

9. Bake the cake for 45 minutes. Test it by sticking a skewer into it. When it comes out it should have no mixture sticking to it.

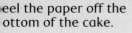

Peel the paper off the bottom of the cake.

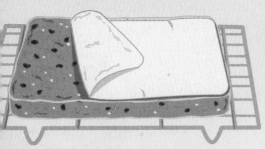

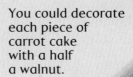

You could decorate each piece of carrot cake with a half a walnut.

10. Leave the cake for ten minutes to cool. Then, run a knife around the sides of the cake and turn the cake out onto a wire rack.

11. While the cake is cooling, sift the powdered sugar into a bowl. Add the cream cheese, lemon juice and vanilla. Beat the mixture well.

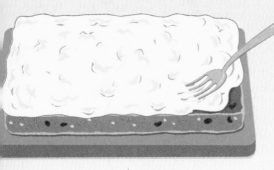

12. When the cake has cooled, spoon the frosting onto it. Spread the frosting with a fork, making lots of swirly patterns.

Rainy day squares

Makes 12 squares

¾ cup margarine
¾ cup brown sugar
2 tablespoons of white corn syrup
2½ cups oatmeal

A 7 x 11in. shallow pan

Preheat your oven to 325°F.

Storage: Keep in an airtight container and eat within a week.

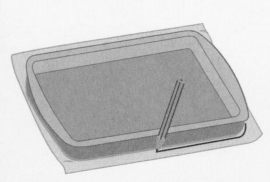

The syrup will slide off a hot spoon more easily than a cold one.

1. Turn on your oven. Put the tin onto greaseproof or wax paper and draw around the bottom of the pan.

2. Cut out the rectangle of paper and put it into the pan. Then, grease it with some margarine on a paper towel.

3. Put the margarine into a large pan and add the sugar. Dip a tablespoon into hot water then use it to add the syrup.

4. Heat the mixture gently, until the margarine has melted. Stir it with a wooden spoon, but don't allow the mixture to boil.

5. Take the pan off the heat. Then, add the oatmeal. Stir them in really well so that they are covered in the syrup mixture.

6. Spoon the mixture into the pan and spread it all over the bottom. Push the mixture well into the corners.

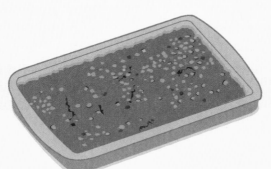

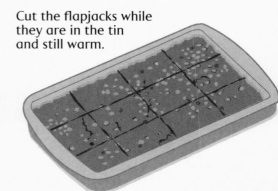

Cut the flapjacks while they are in the tin and still warm.

7. Smooth the mixture with the back of a spoon. Then, put on oven gloves and put the pan on the middle shelf of your oven.

It's best to cut the squares while they are still warm and in the pan.

8. Bake the mixture for about 25 minutes. They are ready when the oatmeal has turned golden brown.

9. Take the pan out of the oven and leave it for ten minutes. Cut the mixture into pieces. Leave them in the pan until they are cold.

Strawberry trifle

Serves four

1lb. fresh strawberries
4 short cakes or sponge cakes
2 tablespoons of strawberry jam
4 tablespoons of apple juice
1 small lemon
1¼ cups heavy cream
3 tablespoons of milk
half a teaspoon of vanilla extract
2 tablespoons of sugar

Storage: The trifle is best eaten on the day you make it, but any leftovers can be covered with plastic foodwrap and stored in the refrigerator for up to two days.

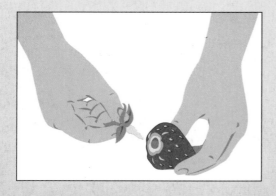

1. Pull the stalks out of the strawberries. Try to pull out them out with the core still attached. Use a small knife if you need to.

Leave a few strawberries for the top of your trifle.

2. Cut most of the strawberries in half, or in quarters if they are very big. Put the pieces into a medium-sized bowl.

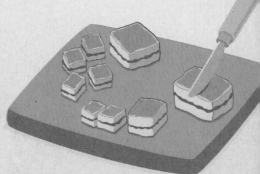

3. Cut the cake into pieces. Spread each half with jam then press them back together again. Cut the cake into smaller pieces.

4. Put the pieces of cake on top of the strawberries and mix them gently. Trickle the apple juice over them.

5. Cover the bowl with plastic food wrap and put it into the refrigerator for about three hours. The cake will soften.

6. Grate the yellow rind, or zest, from the lemon, using the medium holes on a grater. Then, use a knife to scrape off the zest.

7. When the cake mixture is nearly chilled, put the cream into a large bowl. Add the milk, lemon zest, vanilla and sugar.

8. Beat the mixture with a whisk until it becomes slightly stiff. Don't beat it too hard as it will become too solid to spread.

9. Spread the creamy mixture over the cake and strawberries. Put the trifle in the refrigerator until you are ready to serve it.

Instead of making the trifle in one bowl, you can make individual servings in smaller bowls.

Macaroni and cheese

Serves four

1 cup dried macaroni

For the cheese sauce:
4 tablespoons butter
4 tablespoons flour
2²/₃ cups milk
6oz. grated Cheddar cheese
salt and pepper

For the topping:
1oz. grated Cheddar cheese

Preheat your oven to 350°F.

🦋 Eat immediately.

Serve the macaroni and cheese with the garden salad from pages 24-25.

Pour the macaroni back into the pan after it has drained.

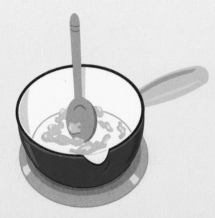

Add a pinch of salt and pepper too.

1. Turn on your oven. Put the macaroni into a pan. Cook it following the instructions on its package. Drain it when it's cooked.

2. To make the sauce, melt the butter in a pan over a low heat. Stir in the flour with a wooden spoon and cook it for one minute.

3. Take the pan off the heat and add a little milk. Stir it really well. Continue stirring in the rest of the milk, a little at a time.

4. Return the pan to the heat and start to bring it to a boil, stirring all the time. The sauce will stick if you don't stir it.

5. The sauce will begin to thicken. Let the sauce bubble for a minute then turn off the heat. Stir in the cheese.

6. Pour the sauce over the cooked macaroni. Stir it really well so that the sauce coats all of the pieces of macaroni.

7. Dip a paper towel into some margarine and rub it inside an ovenproof dish to grease it. Pour in the cheesy macaroni.

8. Sprinkle on grated cheese for the topping. Put the dish into the oven for about 25 minutes, until the top is golden brown.

Chocolate brownies

Makes 15 brownies

¾ cup margarine
1 ⅔ cups sugar
1 teaspoon of vanilla extract
3 eggs
1 cup flour
1 level teaspoon of baking powder
1 cup cocoa
6oz. walnuts*

a 9 x 12in. pan

Preheat your oven to 350°F.

Storage: Keep in an airtight container
and eat within a week.

* Don't give these to anyone who is allergic to nuts.

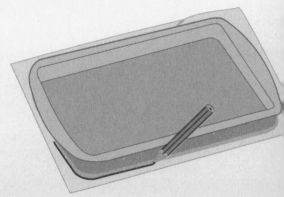

1. Put your pan onto a piece of greaseproof or wax paper. Draw around it and cut out the rectangle.

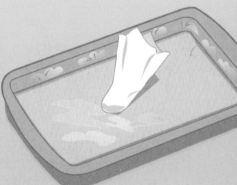

2. Grease the pan with some margarine on a paper towel. Lay the paper in the pan and grease the top of it. Turn on your oven.

3. Put the margarine into a pan and melt it over a low heat. Pour it into a mixing bowl, then add the sugar and vanilla.

Beat the mixture each time you add some egg.

4. Break the eggs into a small bowl and beat them. Add them to the large bowl, a little at a time. Beat them in well.

5. Sift the flour into the bowl and add the baking powder and the cocoa. Stir everything together so that it is mixed well.

6. Put the walnuts onto a chopping board and cut them into small pieces. Add them to the mixture and stir it well again.

7. Pour the mixture into the pan and smooth the top with the back of a spoon. Bake it for about 40 minutes.

Use a spatula to lift them.

8. The brownies are ready when they have risen and a crust has formed on top. They should still be soft in the middle.

9. Leave the brownies in the pan for five minutes, then cut them into 15 squares. Leave them on a wire rack to cool.

Poppy's favorite chocolate cake

Makes about 12 slices

2 teaspoons of vegetable oil
1¾ cups self-rising flour
6 tablespoons of cocoa powder
2 teaspoons of baking powder
1½ cups sunflower margarine (not
   low-fat spread)
2¼ cups soft brown sugar
2 teaspoons of vanilla extract
6 large eggs

For the frosting:
5oz. German chocolate bar
1 cup whipping cream

Two 8in. round cake pans

Preheat your oven 325°F.

Storage: This is best eaten
on the day you make it.

1. Turn on your oven. Put
the cake pans onto
greaseproof or wax paper
and draw around them.
Cut out the circles.

Use a
pastry
brush.

2. Brush vegetable oil over
the inside of the pans. Put
a paper circle in the
bottom of each one, then
brush the paper with oil.

3. Hold a sifter over a
large bowl and sift the
flour, cocoa and baking
powder through it. Get out
another mixing bowl.

Use a
wooden
spoon.

4. Put the margarine and
sugar into the empty bowl
and beat until they are
creamy. Add the vanilla
and beat it again.

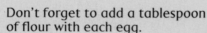
Don't forget to add a tablespoon
of flour with each egg.

5. Crack one egg into a
cup and add it to the bowl
with one tablespoon of
flour. Beat well. Repeat
this with each egg.

6. Gently stir in the rest of
the flour, moving the
spoon in the shape of a
number eight. This will
keep the mixture light.

Use a knife to make the top level.

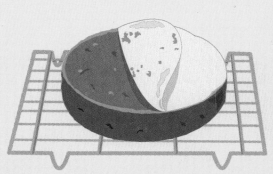

7. Put the mixture into the cake pans. Put them on the middle shelf of the oven. Cook for 40-45 minutes. Test them with a skewer.

8. When the cakes are cooked, leave them to cool for five minutes. Then, run a knife around the side of each pan.

9. Turn each pan upside down over a wire rack and shake it. The cakes should pop out. Peel off the paper and leave them to cool.

10. For the frosting, break the chocolate into a heat-proof bowl. Add the cream. Heat 2in. of water in a pan until it starts to bubble.

11. Put the bowl in the pan. Stir the chocolate as it melts. When it has melted, let it cool, then put the bowl into the refrigerator.

12. Stir the frosting a few times while it is cooling in the refrigerator. It will thicken. When it is like soft butter, take it out of the refrigerator.

The cake is very rich, so don't cut it into huge slices.

13. Spread a third of the frosting on one cake. Put the other cake on top of it and cover the top and sides with the frosting.

Picnic cookies

Makes about 12 cookies

¼ cup sugar
½ cup brown sugar
½ cup butter (not low-fat spread)
1 egg
half a teaspoon of vanilla extract
1 cup, 2 tablespoons flour
6oz. chocolate chips

Preheat your oven to 350°F

✿ Storage: Keep in an airtight
container and eat within five days

1. Grease two baking sheets by dipping a paper towel into butter or margarine. Rub it over the baking sheets. Turn on your oven.

2. Put the sugar, brown sugar and the butter into a large mixing bowl. Stir them together really well with a wooden spoon.

3. Continue stirring them together briskly. You are trying to get the mixture as smooth and creamy as you can.

4. Break the egg into a small bowl and beat it well. Pour the vanilla into a measuring spoon, then mix it in with the egg.

Use a wooden spoon.

5. Pour the eggy mixture into the mixing bowl and stir it in. Then, sift the flour into the bowl and stir the mixture.

6. When you have a smooth mixture, stir in 4oz. of the chocolate chips. You'll use the rest of them later.

7. Put a heaped tablespoon of the mixture onto a baking sheet. Use up the rest of the mixture to make eleven more cookies.

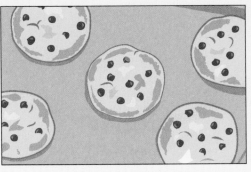

8. Flatten each cookie slightly with the back of a fork. Sprinkle the top of each one with some of the remaining chocolate chips.

9. Bake the cookies for 10-15 minutes, until they are pale golden brown. They should still be slightly soft in the middle.

10. Leave the cookies for a few minutes, then use a spatula to lift them onto a wire rack. Leave them to cool.

Orange cookies

Makes about 60 cookies

¾ cup butter
1¾ cups all-purpose flour
quarter of a teaspoon of salt
2 teaspoons of baking powder
1 large egg
1 cup sugar
1 teaspoon of vanilla extract
2 oranges

Preheat your oven to 400°F.

Storage: Keep in an airtight container for up to five days. This makes a lot of cookies, but you don't need to use it all at once (see step 9).

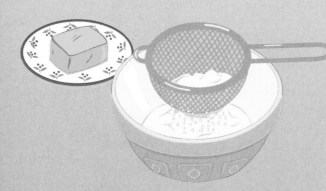

1. Measure the butter and leave it for about an hour to soften. Sift the flour, salt and baking powder into a bowl.

2. Break the egg into a cup or small bowl. Beat it briskly with a fork, so that the yolk and the white are mixed well.

3. Put the butter and sugar into another bowl and beat them until they are creamy. Stir in the egg and the vanilla.

Scrape the zest off the grater with a knife.

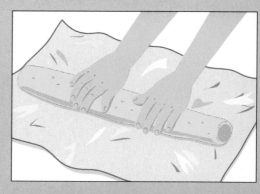

4. Grate the skin, or zest, off the oranges using the medium holes on a grater. Stir the zest into the creamy mixture.

5. Add the flour and stir it until you get a smooth dough. If the dough feels very soft, put it into the refrigerator for an hour.

6. Put a long piece of foil onto your work surface and scrape the dough onto it. Roll the dough to make a long sausage shape.

: Wrap the foil around
he dough and put it in
he refrigerator for about
n hour, until it becomes
irm. Turn on your oven.

. Take the dough out of
he refrigerator and cut
into very thin slices.
ou don't need to use all
he dough at one time.

9. If you don't want to use
all the dough, wrap it in foil.
It will keep for about ten
days in the refrigerator or
up to six weeks in a freezer.

. Spread out the slices of
ough on a non-stick
aking sheet. Bake them
or about seven minutes,
ntil they are golden.

11. Leave the cookies on
the baking sheet for one
minute, then use a spatula
to slide them onto a wire
rack to cool.

Bread rolls

Makes 16 roll

4¼ cups wheat or strong white bread flou
1½ teaspoons of sal
2 teaspoons of suga
1½ teaspoons of rapid rise dried yeas
1 cup, 2 tablespoons mill
2 tablespoons butte
1 egg

Two baking sheets, grease

Preheat your oven to 425°F

 These are best eaten o
the day you make them

You can sprinkle poppy seeds or sesame seeds onto the rolls after brushing them with egg (see step 11).

1. Shake the flour and salt through a sifter into a larg bowl. Stir in the sugar and yeast, then make a hollow in the middle.

Stir it with a wooden spoon.

The mixture should be lukewarm, not hot.

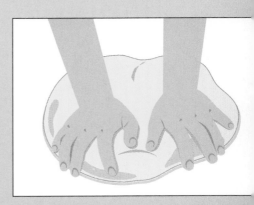

2. Put the milk and butter into a pan and heat it very gently until the butter has just melted. Take the pan off the heat.

3. Pour the milk mixture into the hollow in the flour. Stir it until it is all mixed and no longer sticks to the side of the bowl.

4. Sprinkle some flour onto a clean, dry work surface. Knead the dough by pushing it away from you with both hands.

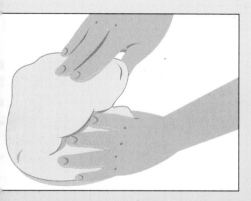

. Fold the dough in half
nd turn it around. Then
ush it away from you
gain. This is called
neading.

6. Knead the dough until it
is smooth and elastic. Dip
a paper towel in oil, then
rub it inside a bowl. Put
the dough in the bowl.

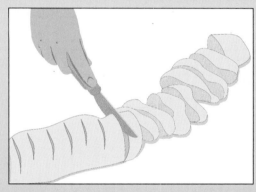

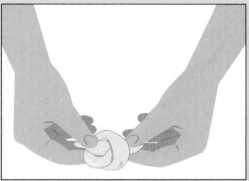

. Cover the bowl with
lastic wrap. Leave it in a
warm place for about 45
minutes, until the dough
as risen to twice its size.

8. Knead the dough again
for about a minute, to
burst any large bubbles
of air in it. Then, divide
the dough into 16 pieces.

9. Roll each piece of dough
to make a 'sausage' about
10in. long. Tie each one
into a knot and put it on a
greased baking sheet.

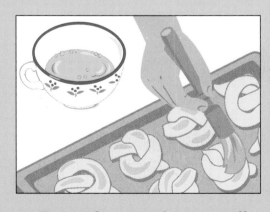

The rolls
will
become
golden
brown.

o. Turn on your oven. Rub
ome plastic wrap with oil,
hen cover the rolls. Put
hem back in a warm place
or 20 minutes.

11. Beat the egg in a small
bowl, then take the plastic
wrap off the rolls. Brush
each roll with some of the
beaten egg.

12. Bake the rolls for 10-12
minutes. Leave them on
the baking sheets for a few
minutes, then leave them
to cool on a wire rack.

Cooking tips

If you haven't done much cooking before, some of the cooking techniques in this book may be new to you, so you may need some help. These two pages explain some of the cooking words which are used in the book.

Measuring spoons

Use measuring spoons to measure ingredients in tablespoons or teaspoons. They give you exactly the amount you need.

Sifting

You need to sift some ingredients, such as flour, to get rid of lumps. Put the flour in a sifter over a bowl and gently shake the sifter.

Adding eggs

When a recipe asks you to add eggs to a mixture, break them into a cup or small bowl first, then add them to the mixture.

Rubbing in

1. Use a blunt knife to mix pieces of margarine or butter with the flour. Stir and cut until the pieces are coated with flour.

2. Then, rub the pieces between your fingertips. As you rub, lift the mixture up and let it fall back into the bowl.

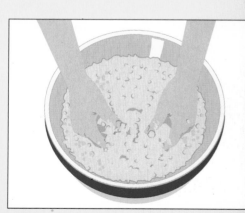

3. Continue rubbing in the butter or margarine until i is completely mixed in and the mixture looks like fine breadcrumbs.

Beating an egg

Break the egg into a cup or small bowl. Use a fork to stir it quickly until the white and the yolk are mixed together.

Beating a mixture

1. When you beat a mixture, you mix the ingredients really well. First, put the ingredients into a big bowl.

2. Then, stir the ingredients briskly, using a wooden spoon. Continue until the mixture is smooth and has no lumps in it.

Lining and greasing a cake pan

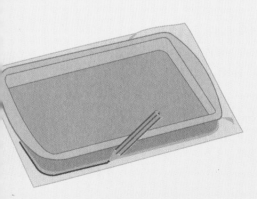

Put the pan onto a piece of greaseproof or wax paper. Use a pencil to draw around the bottom of the pan.

This stops the mixture from sticking.

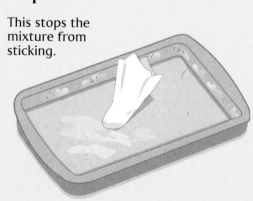

2. Cut out the shape you drew and put it into the pan. Dip a paper towel into some margarine or butter and rub it over to grease the pan.

Testing a cake

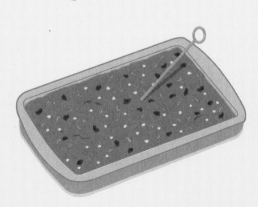

To see if a cake is cooked, push a skewer or toothpick into it. There should be no mixture sticking to the skewer when you pull it out.

Index

Photographic manipulation by John Russell. Thanks to Kate Fearn, Vici Leyhane and Antonia Miller.

First published in 2002 by Usborne Publishing Ltd, 83-85 Saffron Hill, London ECiN 8RT, England. www.usborne.com
Printed in Spain. First published in America 2003. AE

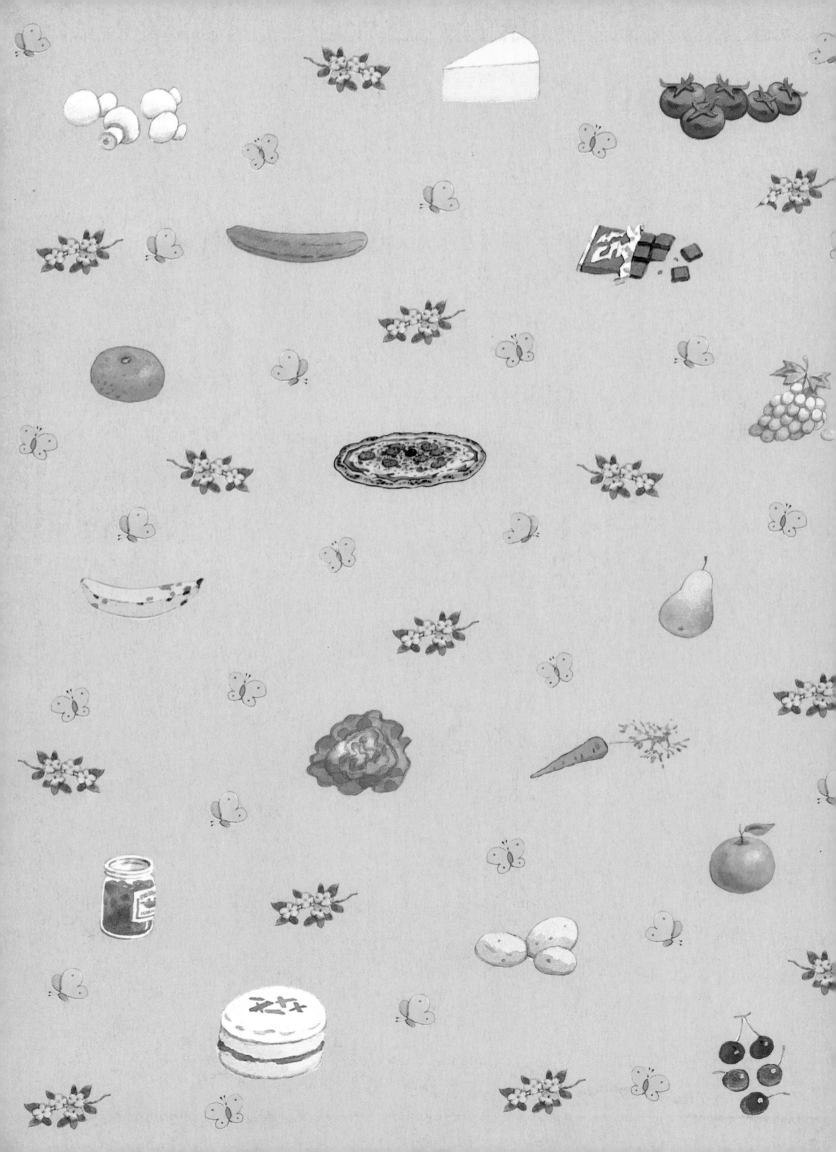